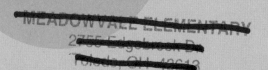

A Note to Parents and Caregivers:

Read-it! Readers are for children who are just starting on the amazing road to reading. These beautiful books support both the acquisition of reading skills and the love of books.

The PURPLE LEVEL presents basic topics and objects using high frequency words and simple language patterns.

The RED LEVEL presents familiar topics using common words and repeating sentence patterns.

The BLUE LEVEL presents new ideas using a larger vocabulary and varied sentence structure.

The YELLOW LEVEL presents more challenging ideas, a broad vocabulary, and wide variety in sentence structure.

The GREEN LEVEL presents more complex ideas, an extended vocabulary range, and expanded language structures.

The ORANGE LEVEL presents a wide range of ideas and concepts using challenging vocabulary and complex language structures.

When sharing a book with your child, read in short stretches, pausing often to talk about the pictures. Have your child turn the pages and point to the pictures and familiar words. And be sure to reread favorite stories or parts of stories.

There is no right or wrong way to share books with children. Find time to read with your child, and pass on the legacy of literacy.

Adria F. Klein, Ph.D.
Professor Emeritus
California State University
San Bernardino, California

Editor: Christianne Jones
Designer: Nathan Gassman
Page Production: Michelle Biedscheid
The illustrations in this book were created digitally.

Picture Window Books
5115 Excelsior Boulevard
Suite 232
Minneapolis, MN 55416
877-845-8392
www.picturewindowbooks.com

Printed in the United States of America.

All books published by Picture Window Books
are manufactured with paper containing at least
10 percent post-consumer waste.

Library of Congress Cataloging-in-Publication Data
Shaskan, Trisha Speed, 1973-
Ava the angelfish / by Trisha Speed Shaskan ; illustrated by James Mackey.
p. cm. — (Read-it! readers)
ISBN 978-1-4048-4079-9 (library binding)
[1. Angelfish—Fiction. 2. Coral reef animals—Fiction. 3. Coral reefs and islands—
Fiction. 4. Birthdays—Fiction.] I. Mackey, James, 1979- ill. II. Title.
PZ7.S53242Av 2008
[E]—dc22   2007032898

Ava the Angelfish

by Trisha Speed Shaskan

illustrated by James Mackey

Special thanks to our reading adviser:

Adria F. Klein, Ph.D.
Professor Emeritus, California State University
San Bernardino, California

PiCTURE WINDOW BOOKS
Minneapolis, Minnesota

Ava woke up early. It was her birthday.
She was three years old.

Ava couldn't wait to see her friends.

Ava swam near the top of the coral reef. The water was warm from the sunlight.

"Goby?" she called out. Goby did not answer.

Ava swam to the side of the coral reef.
It was a fun place to play hide-and-seek.

"Seahorse?" she called out.
Seahorse did not answer.

Ava swam down to the sandy bottom.
It was the best place to take a nap.

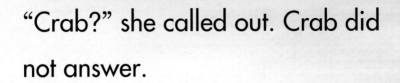

"Crab?" she called out. Crab did not answer.

Ava swam past her favorite rock.
It looked like a castle.

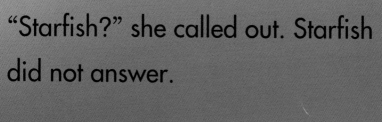

"Starfish?" she called out. Starfish did not answer.

Ava was sad. Where were all of her friends?

Goby swam out of the top of the coral reef. Seahorse swam out of the side.

Crab crawled out of the sand. Starfish climbed off a rock.

"Surprise!" yelled Goby, Seahorse, Crab, and Starfish.

Ava and her friends ate seaweed cake.

Then they opened gifts and played tag.

Ava had a fun birthday.

More *Read-it!* Readers

Bright pictures and fun stories help you practice your reading skills. Look for more books at your level.

On the Web

FactHound offers a safe, fun way to find Web sites related to topics in this book. All of the sites on FactHound have been researched by our staff.

1. Visit *www.facthound.com*

2. Type in this special code:
   1404840799

3. Click on the FETCH IT button.

Your trusty FactHound will fetch the best sites for you!
A complete list of *Read-it!* Readers is available on our Web site:
www.picturewindowbooks.com